Destin... Planet Blobb

Written by Jill Eggleton
Illustrated by Dave Gunson

Rigby

AND

have arrived on Planet
Blobb at the end of
their long trip from
another planet.
They are on vacation.

Read on and you can
join their trip, too.

2

Inside the spaceport

ZENA AND ZOLTA

send a message home:

DV SZEV OZMWVW
LM KOZMVG YOLYY.
OLEV UILN
AVMZ ZMW ALOGZ.

4

WELCOME TO PLANET BLOBB

ARRIVALS

SPACESHIP	TIME OF ARRIVAL
EARTH 223	JUNE 2
MOON ROCKET 42	AUGUST 5
GALAXY BUS 681	DECEMBER 8
MARSCAR 842	DECEMBER 28

BLOBBCODE

This is the Blobb language. You must send all messages to other planets in this code.

A – Z	J – Q	S – H
B – Y	K – P	T – G
C – X	L – O	U – F
D – W	M – N	V – E
E – V	N – M	W – D
F – U	O – L	X – C
G – T	P – K	Y – B
H – S	Q – J	Z – A
I – R	R – I	

START   **END**

DEPARTING PASSENGERS

ZENA

SEND MESSAGE

TODAY'S WEATHER

RAIN	NO
SNOW	NO
FLOODS	NO
THUNDERSTORMS	NO
BLOBBQUAKES	NO
DUST STORMS	YES
WIND SPEED	20 mph

100 DEGREES
BELOW
FREEZING

NO ALIENS
PAST HERE

AIRSHIPS
THIS WAY

EXIT TO
BLOBB CITY

WAIT
HERE FOR
BLOBB CITY
SHUTTLE

VISITORS'
CENTER

DO NOT ENTER

7

TAKE CARE AT ALL TIMES. Wheels can skid very easily.

At the Visitors' Center,

ZENA

ZOLTA

AND

take a space buggy to see the sights.

BLOBB BUGGY HIRE

CHECKLIST

DO NOT DRIVE OFF IN A BUGGY UNLESS YOU HAVE:

- ☑ *BATTERIES*
- ☑ *SOLAR CELLS*
- ☑ *REPAIR KIT*
- ☑ *RADIO*
- ☑ *FOOD*
- ☑ *WATER*

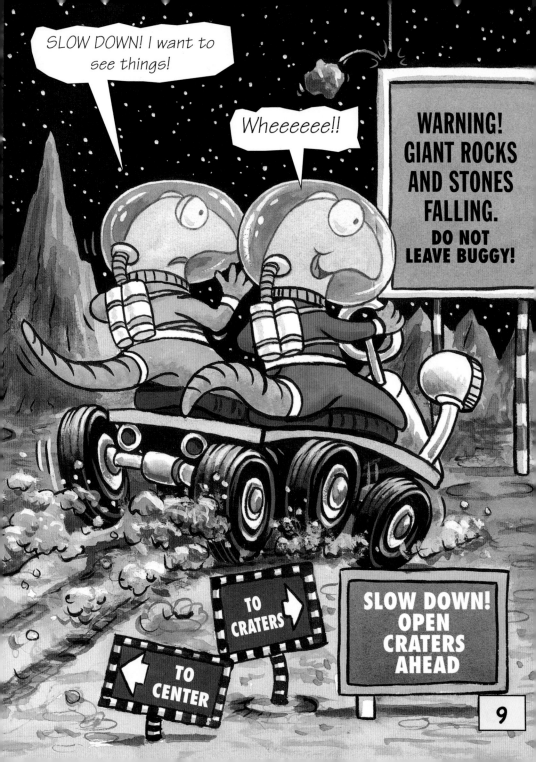

Then an airship trip takes

AND

over the Grand Crater.

BLOBB TOURS INFORMATION

Distance to Earth:
200 billion miles
Travel time:
3 years
Distance to Galaxy Center:
500 billion miles
Travel time:
7.5 years
Distance to nearest Black Hole:
700 billion miles
Travel time:
10.5 years

GRAND CRATER

This is the biggest crater on Planet Blobb.

It is 40 times wider and twice as deep as any hole in the galaxy.

Scientists think it was made by an enormous meteorite.

11

Welcome to ZORTON

ZORTON was built in 2027. It was the first city built on a planet other than Earth. Everything is underground. The roof of the city is covered with soil to act as a shield and to protect people from dangerous rays. There are no windows because there is no fresh air or bright sunlight on Planet Blobb.

Look at these carts. They have a computer. I think we have to put in a code for where we want to go.

TRAVEL CARTS

There's the code.

BLOBB CITY	BBC
LIBRARY	LIB
HOSPITAL	HOS
SUPERMARKET	SUP
CITY PARK	CPK
SPACEBOARD PARK	SPK

ZOLTA

B07

B07

At the Zorton
Supermarket

ZENA **AND** ZOLTA

look for a place with
their favorite food.

ZORTON SUPERMARKET FOOD DEPARTMENT

FOOD	CODE	FOOD	CODE
QUIZZLES	QZ	FLOOPLOOPS	FP
SQUIRTS	SQ	TIGGYOGGIES	TG
BUTTIES	BT	SPROGS	SG
GLOBSY	GS	UGTARTS	UT
BLIKKA	BK	SPLATS	SP
IKFLAKES	IF	GUNGE	GN
PLOPS	PP	JOLLYLIGGLES	JG
MOKBERRIES	PK	FLIPCAKES	FC
POKLICK	SC	BITTLES	BT
SCOUSE	PZ	OOZEPIES	OZ
SPUFFS	SF	BLOBBUPS	BB
SNUKS	SK	GRAPPLES	GP
AKBALLS	AB	LUMPKIN	LP
OGGS	OG	DOODLES	DD
SPUTS	SP	ZATSAUSE	ZS
ZURGLOOS	ZL	WOPWOPS	WW
⌐TROTS	PR	GLURGLES	GG
	QQ	MUSH	MH
	NO	FLUMPS	FP
	IK	SIZZLES	SZ
	UZ	OOMPHS	OO
	PA	ZONK	ZK

15

But the place that

AND

like the best is the spaceboard park.

STOP! We passed the picturephone. Let's phone home. They will want to know if we are having a good time.

SIGNS

Signs give information in a short message.

Signs can: WARN   Direct ⇨
Describe   Instruct

How to write a sign ▶

Step **1** Decide on the PURPOSE of the sign.
Think about the AUDIENCE.

Step **2** Decide on the MESSAGE.
List the KEY WORDS.

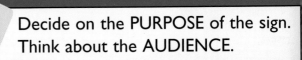

STOP spacesuit
DO NOT LEAVE
wearing

Step **3** THINK about the VISUALS that would help make your message CLEARER for the reader.

You could use ARROWS ⟶

SYMBOLS ⟶

Step 4

DESIGN your sign. Think about adding IMPACT to your key words.

Think about:

FONT SIZE A A **A** **A**   FONT COLOR A A **A** **A**

SHAPE of words.

WHERE the words will be placed.

Step 5

CHECK your sign.
Is the message CLEAR?
Can you ADD anything?
Can you TAKE OUT anything?

*CODES give messages, too, by using a different system of symbols or letters.

BLOBB CODE YOLYY XLWV*

A – Z	H – S	O – L	V – E
B – Y	I – R	P – K	W – D
C – X	J – Q	Q – J	X – C
D – W	K – P	R – I	Y – B
E – V	L – O	S – H	Z – A
F – U	M – N	T – G	
G – T	N – M	U – F	

Use this code to solve the messages on pages 4 and 17.

19

■■■ Guide Notes

Title: Destination Planet Blobb
Stage: Fluency (3)

Text Form: Codes and Signs
Approach: Guided Reading
Processes: Thinking Critically, Exploring Language, Processing Information
Written and Visual Focus: Sending Messages

THINKING CRITICALLY
(sample questions)
- What sign do you think Zena and Zolta might look for at first on their arrival at Planet Blobb?
- Look at pages 8 and 9. Why do you think these signs are necessary?
- What is different about the signs on pages 10 and 11 compared to the signs on pages 8 and 9?
- Why do you think the Zorton Supermarket used codes for the food?

EXPLORING LANGUAGE

Terminology
Spread, author, illustrator, credits, imprint information, ISBN number

Vocabulary
Clarify: airlock, docking, spaceport, sealed, degrees, shuttle, solar cells, craters, galaxy, meteorite, shield, department, rays
Pronouns: we, you, I, it
Adjectives: *giant* rocks, *enormous* meteorites, *dangerous* rays
Adverb: skid *easily*
Homonyms: read/reed, wait/weight, not/knot, rays/raise
Antonyms: exit/entrance, leave/enter, arriving/departing
Synonyms: ahead/in front, directs/instructs, nearest/closest

Print Conventions
Colon, apostrophe – possessive (Visitors' Center, today's weather)